✅ S0-AFV-662

Disney Adventures

One-Minute Mysteries

THE CASE OF THE

MYSTERIOUS MOUSE

AND 12 OTHER ANIMAL MYSTERIES

Written by Heather Mitchell
Illustrated by Scott Angle

SCHOLASTIC INC.
New York   Toronto   London   Auckland   Sydney
Mexico City   New Delhi   Hong Kong   Buenos Aires

All stories by Heather Mitchell, with the exception of
The Case of the Dastardly Dog, which is by Brian M. Raftery.

Published by Scholastic Inc., 557 Broadway, New York, NY 10012
by arrangement with Disney Licensed Publishing. SCHOLASTIC and associated
logos are trademarks and/or registered trademarks of Scholastic Inc.

ISBN 0-439-56169-8

12 11 10 9 8 7 6 5 4 3 2 1   3 4 5 6 7 8/0

Printed in the U.S.A.
First Scholastic printing, October 2003

CASE CONTENTS

WHAT'S A ONE-MINUTE MYSTERY?

Got a minute?

*O*ne–*Minute Mysteries* are quick, easy to read whodunnits. They started as a feature in *Disney Adventures magazine*, but they became so popular, we thought they deserved their own series of books.

Here are 13 One-Minute Mysteries, all featuring animals. In this collection, you'll turn into a detective faster than you can turn the page. Read one or two at a time, or if you're feeling super-sleuthy, you can read the entire book at once! In any *case*, read on to be amazed and amused by the antics of some awesome animal acquaintances!

THE CASE OF THE CRIMINAL CATERPILLAR

#1

**How did Legs escape from
the jail in Bug Junction?**

THE CHARACTERS

Buzz Bixby:
A dragonfly detective

Lenny "Legs" Larson:
A crooked caterpillar

Nellie Gnat: *A gnat
police secretary*

Detective Buzz Bixby had solved plenty of big-time cases in Bug Junction—from taking down the famous gangster Molly Mantis to rescuing the beautiful movie star Honey Bee Mine from the evil clutches of the Yellow Jacket Gang. But there was one criminal mastermind who had been keeping Detective Bixby up at night for the last twelve days: The notorious jewel thief, Lenny "Legs" Larson.

Legs was behind every recent jewel heist in town, and he always escaped, only to show up again when the cops were least expecting him. After cleaning up the rest of the crime in the city, Detective Bixby had made it his mission to bring Legs to justice.

Late one night when Buzz was out on the beat, he got a call from Nellie Gnat down at police headquarters.

"Buzz!" Nellie said, "We just got a call in from an eyewitness—Legs Larson is holding up the jewelry store at Twelfth and Vine! You could catch him red-handed if you hurry!"

"Will do, Nellie," Buzz replied. "And thanks for the tip!" With that, Buzz rushed to the scene of the crime, where Legs was still stuffing jewels into a big backpack.

"I've got you now, Larson!" Buzz said, as he caught Legs in the act. "Put all of your hands in the air!"

Triumphant at last, the detective brought the infamous jewel thief back to the police station in several sets of handcuffs. "Look who I found!" Buzz called out to Nellie as he brought Legs in to be booked.

"I know how long you've been waiting to see Legs Larson put in jail, Buzz," Nellie Gnat said. "So if I were you, I'd put him in cell Z, for safe-keeping." She turned back to her desk to start filling

---

YOU'RE BUGGING ME

➤ Did you know that a caterpillar grows to be about 27,000 times the size it was when it first hatched out of its egg?

➤ Caterpillars eat all day long, but they're very picky eaters—most caterpillars will only eat the leaves of the plant they were hatched on!

➤ Did you know that a dragonfly's life span is about six months, but most of that time is spent as a larva underwater?

out forms on Legs's criminal history.

"I think you're absolutely right about that, Nellie. So Legs, how'd you like to spend the night in Bug Junction's toughest jail cell?"

"Your toughest cell doesn't scare me, Detective," said Legs. "I'll bust out of it by morning."

"We'll see about that," Buzz replied. "You haven't seen cell Z yet!"

Buzz walked Legs down the corridor to the last cell on the left, where a ladder poked up from floor to ceiling. "Climb down the ladder and you'll find your bed for the night," said Buzz.

The ladder led twenty feet down to a small cell with a bed and a sink. The only window was an open skylight in the ceiling. When Legs reached the bottom of the ladder, Detective Bixby pulled it up out of the cell, and locked the heavy cell door.

"Good night, Legs—I'll see you tomorrow morning at nine A.M. sharp."

✣ ✣ ✣ ✣

When Nellie and Buzz returned to cell Z in the morning, the cell was locked, but Legs was gone!

"How could he have escaped?" Detective Bixby cried.

"Oh, no!" cried Nellie. "After filling out those forms on Legs last night, I'm afraid I know the answer to that question!"

How did Legs escape?

THE ANSWER

Legs Larson had been a jewel thief for twelve days—about the same amount of time a caterpillar needs before it weaves a cocoon and becomes a butterfly. While locked up in cell Z, Legs had turned into a butterfly and flown out of the open skylight to freedom. Fortunately, however, Buzz and Nellie nabbed him at the train station that afternoon as he was trying to get out of town.

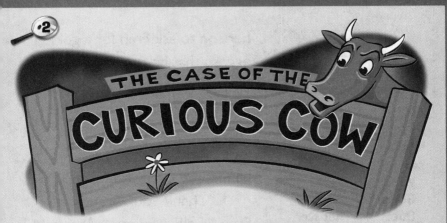

THE CASE OF THE CURIOUS COW

Who grabbed the golden egg-laying goose?

THE CHARACTERS

Farmer Fran Frampton: *The owner of Frampton Farm*

Gilda: *A goose*

Felix Frampton: *Fran Frampton's eight-year-old grandson*

Harold: *A horse*

Chelsea: *A chicken*

Carrie: *A cat*

Whenever anyone in Jasper Village needed new shoes or a bigger house or a nicer overcoat in the winter, they knew who to ask: Fran Frampton. She'd raised flocks of geese on Frampton Farm for more than forty years. All of her geese were beautiful, well-behaved animals, but Fran was famous for one fantastic goose—Gilda, a goose who laid golden eggs.

One late-summer morning, Fran Frampton's grandson, Felix, came to visit the farm. It was almost time for school to start again, and Felix's mother had sent

FARMYARD FACTS

Geese make good "watchdogs"—they will honk at strangers and chase them away from their owners' house!

her son to ask Fran for a golden egg, so that he could afford to buy his pencils and notebooks.

"Why, Felix," Fran said when she opened the door, "you look a foot taller and more handsome every time I see you!"

"Thank you, Grandma Fran," Felix replied. "Mom said I should ask you for a golden egg to help pay for my school supplies."

"Well, that certainly is putting one of Gilda Goose's eggs to good use," Fran reasoned. "Why don't you go ask her for one?"

Felix ran down to the lake and found all the farm animals milling around, making a commotion by the water. "What's wrong?" Felix asked Harold, a tall white horse.

"It's terrible," Harold replied, as he stamped his hooves. "Gilda's been kidnapped!"

"That's ridiculous," said Chelsea the chicken as she walked out from behind the chicken coop. "I was talking to a cow down the road about an hour ago, and he said that he saw Gilda heading off on her own."

"A cow down the road, eh?" said Felix. "What else did she say?"

"He didn't say anything else," Chelsea clucked back. "Just that Gilda looked happy to be on her way."

The animals gasped. "Do you think she's been unhappy all these years?" asked Carrie the cat. "Do you think she wanted to keep her eggs to spend on herself?"

"Makes sense to me," Chelsea replied. "I say we all try to forget her. There's no sense in dwelling on the past."

"If Gilda had left of her own accord, I'd be happy to do just that," Felix said to Chelsea. "But I think you know more about her disappearance than you're telling us!"

How did Felix know Chelsea wasn't telling the truth?

THE ANSWER

Chelsea told the farm animals that a cow from the neighboring farm had told her that "he" had seen Gilda walking down the road. However, Felix knows that cows are always female—male cattle are called bulls. When confronted with her mistake, Chelsea confessed that she and the other chickens had kidnapped Gilda, hidden her in the chicken coop, and bound her beak to keep her quiet, because they were jealous that her golden eggs got so much attention.

THE CASE OF THE SQUIRREL'S STOLEN STUFF

Who stole Samantha the squirrel's secret stash?

THE CHARACTERS

Samantha: *A squirrel*

Shelly: *An elderly shrew (shrews look sort of like mice)*

Patty: *A possum*

Rachel: *A raccoon police chief*

It was early November in Wilson's Woods, and the forest animals were gathering the last stash of food to store, which would feed them all winter long. Everybody, that is, except Samantha Squirrel, who had traveled that evening to her secret hiding place with her last mouthful of acorns, only to find that everything she'd worked so hard to save all year was gone.

"My acorns, my seeds, my hazelnuts—everything is missing!" Samantha wailed as she stared into the empty hole in the trunk of the old oak tree at the woods' edge. "It took me months to save up all that food, and now winter is almost here—what will I do?!"

"I remember a winter a few years back," said a

sharp, nasal voice from the roots of the tree. Samantha turned to see Shelly Shrew, one of the forest's oldest citizens, peeking out of her home at the bottom of the oak. "A fall flood washed away my acorns, and I spent the entire winter eating dandelion seeds. Dandelion seeds for months—ugh! I don't care if I never see another dandelion seed as long as I live!"

"At least you had the seeds to get you through the winter," Samantha replied. "Who could have stolen my *entire* stash of food?"

"Well," said Shelly. "It could have been Sammy Snake, from down by the creek. Or Doris Deer, from the glade near that big rock a bit west of here. Stan Skunk likes seeds, but don't tell anyone I said so, because he wants everyone to think he's a carnivore when we all *know* he's an omnivore. Brenda Badger isn't the nuts-and-seeds type, but there was that time a couple of years ago . . ."

As Shelly kept talking, the sun began to set behind the pines of Wilson's Woods.

". . . and then there's Patty Possum," said Shelly. "She's always wandering around in the bushes— probably up to no good."

Samantha perked up. "Patty Possum—I thought I saw her around this tree this morning. In fact, I'm *sure* I did—she must have stolen my food! Shelly, will you come with me to the police station to file a report?"

"Of course I will, dearie," Shelly replied. "This is the most interesting thing to happen in Wilson's Woods since the time Francie Fox ran off with a lone wolf from the next forest over."

Samantha and Shelly headed off toward the police station. As they were about to cross Crenshaw Creek, they heard a rustling in the bushes nearby.

"Who goes there?" Samantha called out.

"It's me," a sleepy voice replied, "Patty Possum."

"Patty Possum, you come out of there right this minute—I know you stole my food!"

"What?" Patty replied as she walked out of the bushes. "I didn't steal anything!"

"We'll see what the police have to say about that!" Shelly said. "We're headed to the station right now, so you'd better come along if you think you can prove you didn't take Samantha's food!"

When Samantha, Shelly, and Patty got to the police station, they headed straight for Police Chief Rachel Raccoon.

"Now, what's this all about?" the chief asked.

"Patty Possum stole my winter stash of food," Samantha said. "I saw her by my tree this morning, and now my food is gone. I want it back!"

QUICK QUIZ

Animals are either **diurnal**, meaning they are awake during the day and asleep at night, or **nocturnal**, meaning they sleep during the day and wake up at night to find their food. Do you know which of these animals are nocturnal?

Owl	Squirrel	Dog
Bat	Deer	Raccoon
Robin	Snake	Rabbit

ANSWER: Owl, Bat, Raccoon

"But I didn't take it!" cried Patty.

Chief Raccoon sighed and looked at the shrew. "Shelly, are you stirring up rumors again?"

"What do you mean?" Shelly asked innocently.

"Well," the chief replied, "I know you love to gossip, and I also know Patty couldn't have stolen Samantha's food this morning." She turned to Samantha. "Are you *sure* you just didn't forget which tree your winter stash is hidden in?"

How did Rachel Raccoon know Patty Possum couldn't have taken Samantha's food?

THE ANSWER

Samantha said she saw Patty near the tree "this morning," but opossums are nocturnal animals. That means Patty sleeps all day and doesn't wake up until nightfall—about the time when Samantha and Shelly walked by her in the bushes. As it turned out, Chief Raccoon was right—Samantha's stash of acorns was untouched . . . in another tree across the forest.

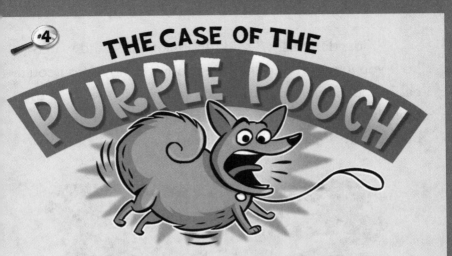

PURPLE POOCH

Who broke Priscilla Pinkerton's precious porcelain pony?

THE CHARACTERS

Penny Pinkerton: *A 13-year-old girl*

Paul Pinkerton: *Penny's 8-year-old brother*

Priscilla and Pat Pinkerton: *Penny and Paul's parents*

Petey Pinkerton: *The Pinkerton's perky Pomeranian (a little, fluffy dog)*

It was Saturday night, and Penny and Paul Pinkerton's parents, Priscilla and Pat, were going out to dinner and a movie.

"Take good care of your little brother, Penny," Mrs. Pinkerton said, "and make sure you two take Petey out for a nice long walk before that show you like so much comes on TV."

Penny sighed and rolled her eyes at her mother. "It's not just *some* show, Mom— it's the *Percy Parker Show!*" Penny flopped down on the sofa and sighed again. "Percy Parker is *sooooo* dreamy."

"*Ewwwwwww,*" said Paul. "You're weird, Penny."

"Kids, don't fight," said Mr. Pinkerton. "And watch how you jump around the living room, Penny—you could easily knock over your mother's favorite statue." On the table behind the sofa, a porcelain statue of a prancing purple pony was proudly displayed.

"Be safe, kids, and have a nice night—we'll be home by ten," Mrs. Pinkerton said. And with that, Priscilla and Pat left.

✧ ✧ ✧ ✧

About an hour later, Penny and Paul were walking Petey around the block when a man in a purple shirt and glasses walked past them eating a sandwich.

"*Bowowowowowowow!*" barked Petey, as he strained at the leash.

A PASSION FOR PURPLE

Purple is a great color! Use this space to write down things you can think of that are purple.

_____
_____
_____
_____
_____
_____

"Easy, boy," Paul said as they walked past the man. "I'm sorry, mister."

Shortly thereafter, the Pinkerton kids passed a girl licking a big purple lollipop. "*Bowowowowowowow!*" barked Petey, pulling at the leash again.

"Wow," Paul said to Penny. "That was weird. I wonder why he started barking like that."

"Whatever," Penny replied. "He just doesn't like strangers, I guess. We'd better hurry and get back, or I'm going to miss the beginning of my show."

❖ ❖ ❖ ❖

ALL ABOUT ANIMALS

➤ Did you know that different kinds of animals see things differently? Most kinds of animals, like dogs and cats, are color-blind—they can only see in black-and-white, and their other senses, like smell and hearing, make their vision less important to them than it is to us.

➤ A small number of other kinds of animals, like monkeys and humans, can see the colors of the rainbow. (Scientists believe that an even smaller number of other kinds of animals and insects, including bees and some kinds of birds, can see even more colors than people can!)

Ten minutes later, the *Percy Parker Show* was starting, and Penny was comfy on the sofa, ready to watch it. But just as the opening credits began, she heard an enormous *CRASH* behind her. She jumped up and saw her mom's statue in pieces on the floor. Paul and Petey stood next to the pile of broken porcelain, looking terrified.

"What happened?" cried Penny.

"Petey just jumped up on the table and knocked down the statue," said Paul. "You saw how he barked at those people on the street—I think he hates the color purple."

Penny sighed. "Mom and Dad are going to be a lot more mad that you broke the statue if you lie about it, Paul," Penny said. "I know Petey doesn't hate the color purple, and so do they."

How did Penny know Paul was lying?

THE ANSWER

Penny knew Petey couldn't hate the color purple, because dogs can only see in black-and-white. When their parents came home, Paul apologized to them for accidentally breaking the statue—and to Petey, whom he'd forgotten to feed any dinner (which is why the dog had barked at the two people he had passed on the street—he had wanted their food)!

THE CASE OF THE BUMBLING BEE

Who buzzed off with Queen Caroline's honey?

THE CHARACTERS

Queen Caroline: *The ruler of a beautiful beehive*

Lucy: *A stylish ladybug*

Charlie: *A hungry caterpillar*

Alvin: *A fun-loving ant*

Marcy, Mary, and Molly: *The Mosquito sisters*

Debbie, Dana, and Betty: *Worker bees*

The Court of Apiaria was a fabulous beehive, with golden floors and walls, and thousands of loyal subjects working hard to make sure their hive was the best place it could possibly be. Ruling over Apiaria was Queen Caroline, a good and generous monarch who always made sure her subjects were happy and had plenty of honey. The hive was always buzzing with activity, but today the bees were especially excited—Queen Caroline was throwing her annual party for the other insects in the tree—Lucy Ladybug, Charlie Caterpillar, Alvin Ant, and the Mosquito sisters: Marcy, Mary, and Molly.

Late that afternoon, two worker bees, Debbie and Dana, were out gathering the last little bits of pollen for the honey to be served at the party that night.

"Do you think Charlie will eat all the honey again this year?" asked Debbie, as she packed the pouches in her back legs full of pollen.

"I don't know, but I bet he'll try," Dana replied as she looked out over the fields of brightly colored flowers all around them. To most, it was just a sunny meadow, but to Dana's bee eyes, the colors of the flowers formed a path that led right back to Apiaria. "We should get back to the hive, Debbie. It looks like the sun is starting to set, and we can't be caught out in the dark."

With that, the two bees flew back to Apiaria, where the pollen they had gathered would soon become sweet, golden honey for the banquet that night.

✣ ✣ ✣ ✣

As the sun slowly set over the hive, Queen Caroline's guests began to arrive. Lucy Ladybug was first, making a dramatic entrance in her red-and-black wings. Next came Charlie Caterpillar, who brought some leaves with him to munch on before dinner. "You know me," he said, "always eating."

Queen Caroline was a gracious hostess. "Oh, that's just the way you caterpillars are," she said, smiling at Charlie as he munched on a leaf tip. "I understand completely."

"Thank you," said Charlie, after he'd swallowed. "I can't wait for dinner. Your honey is more delicious than a fresh green leaf!"

The next to arrive was Alvin Ant, who had buffed his exoskeleton (the outer "shell" of an insect's body) and was looking especially dashing in shiny black. "Queen Caroline, you sure know how to throw a party!" he exclaimed,

BUZZ

➤ Many kinds of flowers only have a scent during the day, because their smell helps to attract bees. If you have roses in your garden, try smelling them in the afternoon sun and again at night—bet they'll smell stronger during the daytime!

➤ Want to see more bees? Bees are attracted to all flowering plants, but their favorite colors seem to be blue and yellow.

➤ Insects don't have voices. All the noises that bees, mosquitoes, and other insects make is the result of the ways they move their wings— whether they rub them together, like a cricket, or just move them so fast the air vibrates around them, like a bee.

looking around
at the dazzling
banquet hall.

"Why, thank
you, Alvin," the
queen replied.
"We'll be able to
start dinner once the
Mosquito sisters arrive,
but I'm afraid they seem to be late."

An hour later, the Mosquito sisters were still
nowhere to be found.

"I'm starving," cried Charlie, who had finished his
leaves long ago. "I'm going back to my house to get
another snack! Go ahead and start dinner without me,
if the Mosquito sisters show up. I'll be back soon."

Almost immediately after Charlie left, there was a
sharp, high-pitched buzzing sound in the night air.

"Oh, good," said Queen Caroline. "The Mosquitoes
are here!"

"So sorry we're late," Marcy Mosquito buzzed, as
she entered the hive.

"There was a breeze blowing outside," Molly
Mosquito added, "and it was hard for us to fly all the way
up here from our puddle at the bottom of the tree."

Queen Caroline was very hungry, but again, she was
a gracious hostess. "Darlings, we didn't even notice the

time. Don't worry about it," she said. "But now that you're here, we can get started. Will everyone take their seats, please?"

As Queen Caroline and her guests moved to the banquet table and sat down, worker bees sprang into action, buzzing off to the kitchen to get the honey.

Just then, Charlie Caterpillar returned to the hive. "I just had a twig with a few buds," he said. "Nothing that will spoil my appetite." He spotted the Mosquito sisters. "Marcy, Mary, Molly! Nice to see you all again!"

Just then, a small, scared-looking worker bee buzzed slowly into the banquet hall. "Qu-qu-queen Caroline?" she stuttered.

"Yes, Betty?" the queen replied.

"The honey," said the worker bee. "It's . . . gone!"

The queen and her guests gasped in horror. "I don't understand," cried the queen. "Who could have done such a horrible thing?"

"Maybe a guest who was too hungry to wait for dinner," Lucy Ladybug said, glaring at Charlie.

OH, BEE-HAVE!

How do bees know where to find the best flowers? They dance! When a bee finds some great flowers, she returns to the hive and starts to dance, shaking her body in the direction of the flowers. Other bees in the hive start dancing along, and soon all of the bees know where to find the flowers. **Can you think of a dance you could do to tell someone something without using words?**

"It wasn't me!" Charlie replied.

"We believe him," Mary Mosquito said.

"We heard bees buzzing away from the hive as we flew up to it," Marcy continued. "It must have been your own worker bees who stole the honey."

"Perhaps they're sick of working so hard for you," Molly added.

Queen Caroline gave the Mosquito sisters a cold look. "You say you heard my workers flying away from the hive?" she said.

"Yes," Marcy replied. "And they sounded like they were leaving fast!"

"I've heard enough," the Queen said. "I know who stole my honey, and I know where it must be."

How did Queen Caroline know who stole the honey?

THE ANSWER

Even though hungry Charlie Caterpillar seemed like the most likely culprit, Queen Caroline knew the Mosquito sisters must have been lying about hearing worker bees leaving the hive. Because bees use the bright colors of flowers and other objects to navigate through the air, they never fly at night. The next morning, the queen sent her worker bees down to the mosquito puddle at the bottom of the tree, where the stolen honey was recovered.

THE CASE OF THE MYSTERIOUS MOUSE

Who snatched the Dazzling Diamond?

THE CHARACTERS

Frau Helga von Squeakenstein:
A wealthy mouse Countess

Herr Hans von Squeakenstein:
Helga's young nephew

Lord Edward Mousebatton: *A noble, outgoing mouse*

Windsor Templeton: *A sad mouse*

William Ratton: *Rodent police commissioner*

For more than one hundred years, mice from around the world had traveled to the basement of the Plaza Hotel in New York City for the highlight of the international rodent social calendar—the annual Mousequerade Masked Ball. On this very special night, thousands of mice travel to New York to dress up in exotic costumes, put on fabulous masks, and dance the night away.

One year, the Grande Dame of the ball was Countess Helga von Squeakenstein, an elderly mouse who lived in the wine cellar of a creepy, old castle in the mountains of Germany. She attended the ball with her nephew, Hans. To match her sparkling silver mask, Frau von Squeakenstein wore the most priceless gem in her vast collection of jewels—the spectacular Dazzling Diamond. It was a huge, tear-shaped stone that could've been seen sparkling enchantingly from hundreds of feet away.

Though beautiful, the Dazzling Diamond had a dark past, and many mice thought it was cursed. No mouse had ever owned the stone for more than twenty years without something awful happening to them, but the Dazzling Diamond was so special that it was never destroyed. And that night it was around Frau von Squeakenstein's neck, glittering in the light of a thousand candles and spinning around the room with her as she danced.

"I say, Frau von Squeakenstein—that necklace is one of the most spectacular I have ever seen," exclaimed Lord Edward Mousebatton, who was dressed as a fierce pirate. He led Frau von Squeakenstein around the dance floor to a stately waltz. "But isn't there some sort of curse on the jewel?" he asked.

"They say the Dazzling Diamond cannot remain in the hands of one mouse for more than twenty years. Mice who have owned the stone for more than twenty years have died, or lost their fortunes," Frau von Squeakenstein replied. "But I will have had the stone twenty years and *one day*, tonight—it was a gift from the

Count in our younger days."

"Well, it is a true treasure," Lord Mousebatton chuckled, "and I, for one, am sorry to see it go—but alas, the song is over!"

Just then, the song ended, and Lord Mousebatton swung the countess into the arms of her next dance partner—her nephew, Hans. "Are you enjoying the ball, darling?" the countess asked.

"Why, yes, Auntie—it's a lovely night, with everyone in their costumes and the music playing so sweetly," Hans replied.

"I thought you might like it—and I love your genie costume!" Frau von Squeakenstein exclaimed. "I'm glad you could come as my guest."

Just then, another dancer cut in on them—the tall and sad-looking Windsor Templeton.

"Windsor—so lovely to see you again," Frau von Squeakenstein exclaimed as they set off across the ballroom floor. She looked at his scaly green costume and matching

mask. "Are you a lizard this year, or a sea monster?"

Windsor sighed. "I'm a dragon, Countess—or at least, I'm supposed to be. I had matching wings and a tail, you see, but unfortunately I left them in the cab."

"You look splendid without them," Frau von Squeakenstien said tactfully, "but I have a green scarf upstairs in my hotel suite, if you'd like to use that for a tail."

"Oh, that isn't necessary," Windsor replied. "Just now, I heard you speaking with Lord Mousebatton about your beautiful necklace. Which one of your relatives will you leave that lovely stone to someday?"

"Oh, Windsor—you know I don't like to speak of such things," Frau von Squeakenstein replied. "But if you must know, I have always envisioned giving the Dazzling Diamond to my niece, Greta, for her eighteenth birthday. Surely you know her—Hans's sister?"

"Yes, yes, we met at last year's ball," Windsor said. "A lovely girl."

"I'm glad you approve," Frau von Squeakenstein laughed, as they spun across the floor.

Just then, the lights went out—and for a moment, the guests became disoriented. Suddenly, a gasp was heard from the dance floor. "My necklace!" Frau von Squeakenstein cried. "Someone has stolen it from me!"

A minute or two later, the lights came back on, and sure enough, the Dazzling Diamond had disappeared.

"We must call the police immediately!" Hans von Squeakenstein declared. "Every minute we waste could make my aunt's necklace harder to find."

When Police Commissioner Ratton was called in, he insisted the thief must have been one of Frau von Squeakenstein's dance partners. "He could have loosened the clasp of the necklace earlier in the evening before snatching it off her neck in the darkness," he said. "Now," he said to Lord Mousebatton, Hans, and Windsor Templeton, "where were each of you when you weren't dancing with the countess?"

Lord Mousebatton spoke first. "Prior to our dance, I spent most of the night at the buffet," he said. "They were serving smoked salmon, you see, and it's my favorite dish."

"I spent the night dancing with a beautiful lady mouse I'd never met before," said Hans. "The only time I left her side was to dance with my aunt, the countess."

"I sat in the corner all night," said Windsor

Templeton sadly. "Countess von Squeakenstein was the only guest who would dance with me."

Commissioner Bratton looked at his three suspects. "All right. I have just one more question to ask," he said. "Hans, can you describe the mouse you danced with, so we can question her?"

"Absolutely," Hans replied. "I know every inch of her beautiful face."

"That's all I needed to know," the Commissioner replied. "Frau von Squeakenstein, I'm going to send some officers to search through Hans's belongings—I believe we will find the missing diamond somewhere in your nephew's suitcases."

How did Commissioner Ratton know that Hans had stolen the diamond?

THE ANSWER

The dance was the Mousequerade Masked Ball, so Hans couldn't have known what his dance partner really looked like. He must have been lying when he told Commissioner Ratton he could remember every detail of her face because if she was masked, he wouldn't have been able to see it. The police searched Hans's room and found the diamond, wrapped in the Countess's green scarf, in his suitcase.

THE CASE OF THE COOK-OFF CAPER

Who stole the stinky slab of Stilton cheese?

THE CHARACTERS

Henri Mousetisse: *A mouse chef*

Maurice Cheesevalier: *A mouse chef*

Madame Fromage: *A seller of stinky cheese*

Marie Meowtoinette: *Madame Fromage's cat and shop assistant*

Chevy Chevre: *A dapper dachshund*

Hubert Le Chien: *A big, blustery bloodhound*

Once a year, the citizens of Dairyville throw an annual cheese fondue festival. This celebration always includes a contest to see who makes the best cheese fondue. This year, the pressure was on the town's two most popular restaurants—Henri Mousetisse's and Maurice Cheesevalier's.

On the morning before the contest, Madame Fromage's cheese shop was packed with customers. Madame Fromage's assistant, Marie, walked around the store, passing out samples of the shop's new English Stilton. A giant wheel of the gourmet cheese stood on a pedestal in the center of the store.

"Madame Fromage," Chevy the dachshund yapped from beneath his beret, "this cheese is delicious, but why is it so very expensive?"

"Well," Madame Fromage replied, "it's a very special cheese that comes all the way from England. Plus, it's extra-stinky!"

"We think it's the *purrrrfect* cheese for any occasion," Marie added.

"Madame Fromage, your shop smells better every time I visit," barked Hubert, a big, friendly bloodhound. He stuck his nose up in the air and sniffed deeply. "I notice you bought the extra wheel of brie that you were telling me about last week."

Madame Fromage laughed. "Hubert, that brie is in the back of my storeroom, all the way in the basement—your sense of smell is truly amazing!"

DOGGONE IT!

➤ A bloodhound's sense of smell is 60 times greater than any other kind of dog! Bloodhounds are considered so reliable that they are sometimes used to pick suspects out of a police line-up. The police let the dog smell something that was at the scene of the crime, and the dog picks the criminal based on the suspect's scent.

➤ Stilton is the name of a town in England, but Stilton cheese has never been made there! Stilton cheese comes from the English counties of Leicestershire, Nottinghamshire, and Derbyshire. It's called Stilton because an innkeeper in Stilton sold the delicious (and very stinky) cheese to hungry travelers.

Just then, a commotion broke out in the street in front of the store. Madame Fromage, Marie, and Hubert ran outside, where rival chefs Henri Mousetisse and Maurice Cheesevalier had gotten into quite an argument.

"My cheddar fondue is a sure thing to win this year's gold medal," bragged Henri. "I've spent the entire year coming up with the best, most delicious fondue recipe Dairyville has ever seen."

"We'll see about that. Your cheddar fondue is no match for my Swiss," Maurice retorted. "It has a secret ingredient that'll knock the judges' socks off!"

"Now, now," Hubert called out. "There's no need for fighting. The judges will decide whose fondue is the best soon enough."

"*Mon dieu!*" ("My God!") cried Madame Fromage as she stepped back into her shop. "My Stilton has been stolen!"

The crowd gasped. Who in Dairyville would steal a wheel of precious stinky cheese?

"How terrible!" said Maurice.

"Whoever stole the cheese should be punished,"

Henri added.

"Who could have done such a thing?" Hubert asked.

"I knew the cheese was worth a lot of money, but I can't believe someone would steal it," said Chevy.

"We were all out here with Henri and Maurice—who could have stolen my cheese?" asked Madame Fromage.

"I don't know the answer," said Marie, "but I know who does."

"What do you mean?" asked Madame Fromage.

"I mean that someone here is lying," Marie replied.

How did Marie know someone was lying—and who stole the Stilton?

THE ANSWER

Hubert had smelled the brie Madame Fromage had been keeping in the basement, so Marie knew that Hubert's powerful nose would have alerted him to the fact that the Stilton was being taken from the store. When confronted, Hubert confessed he had been in cahoots with Henri and Chevy—Henri had found out the stinky Stilton was the secret ingredient in Maurice's Swiss cheese fondue and promised Hubert and Chevy a free dinner for helping to steal it. When everyone's backs were turned during the street argument, Chevy went back into the store and stole the cheese.

THE CASE OF THE KIDNAPPED KITTEN

Who snatched Katie's calico cat?

One night, Carol Kingston came home from work to find her daughter Katie waiting for her on the porch—in tears.

"Mom!" wailed Katie, "I'm so glad you're home!"

"What is it, dear?" Mrs. Kingston asked. "What's wrong?"

"Cammie's gone!" cried Katie.

Cammie was a calico kitten that Katie's mom had rescued from the pound for Katie's birthday a week earlier.

"Well, there's Officer Krumky," Mrs. Kingston said,

pointing to a police car slowly driving down the street. "Maybe she can get to the bottom of all of this."

"Officer!" Mrs. Kingston called.

Officer Krumky got out of her car and walked over to the Kingstons. "What seems to be the trouble here?" she asked.

"Cammie—my kitten—is gone!" Katie cried.

"OK," said Officer Krumky. "Calm down and I'm sure we'll get her back for you. Where did you last see Cammie?"

"She was curled up in her basket on the porch this morning," Katie replied.

"And you shut and locked the gate when you left for school?"

"Yes—and it was still locked when I came home after soccer practice," Katie said.

"What time was that?" asked Officer Krumky.

"Six-thirty," Katie replied. "We've been having long practices all week, because

we've got a big game on Saturday."

"I see," said Officer Krumky. "Well, the next step is for me to ask your neighbors if they've seen anything suspicious—I'll get back to you if I find anything."

"Thank you, Officer," Mrs. Kingston said. "We'll be here."

Officer Krumky walked across the street to Kyle Cartman's house. Kyle was in his front yard, playing with his Great Dane, Biff.

"Hi, Kyle," said Officer Krumky.

"Here to ask me about that kitten?" Kyle replied.

"Actually, I am," said Officer Krumky. "How did you know?"

"Oh, that little girl's been crying about it for hours," Kyle replied. "I couldn't help but overhear."

"Did you see the kitten at all today?" Officer Krumky asked.

"Why, no," Kyle replied, "but I would never notice that kitten either way. Biff here hates cats, and to tell you the truth, so do I—I'm much more of a dog person." Just then, Biff jumped up and put his paws on  Kyle's shoulders. Standing on his hind legs, he was even taller than his owner!

"I can see that," said Officer Krumky. "Well, thanks for your time."

Then Officer Krumky went to the house next door to the Kingstons—Courtney Cresswick's house. Courtney answered the door with red eyes and a runny nose. In one hand, she held a big box of tissues, and in the other was a package of allergy medicine.

"A-*choo*!" Courtney sneezed. "Well, hello Officer— can I help you with something?" she asked.

"Are you all right, Miss Cresswick?" Officer Krumky asked. "I don't mean to be rude, but you look awful."

"Oh, that's OK," Courtney replied. "I know—it's allergy season, and I'm allergic to pets, pollen, peanuts—*everything*. My hay fever has been terrible all spring!"

"Well, I'm here to ask you a few questions about Katie Kingston's cat, which was apparently stolen from the Kingston's yard this afternoon."

"Oh, that's terrible!" said Courtney. "Why, I just saw her playing with that kitten in their front yard yesterday afternoon. I was coming home from my sister's place and I just had to watch. It's the cutest little thing!"

"Do you know of anyone who may have wanted to steal Cammie?" Officer Krumky asked.

"Hmm . . . only Kyle Cartman, across the street,"

Courtney replied. "He hates cats—always has."

"I see," the policewoman said.

Officer Krumky knocked on the Kingstons' door a few minutes later, and Katie opened it.

"Did you get Cammie back?" she asked.

"Not yet," Officer Krumky replied, "but I think I know who took her."

How did Officer Krumky know who stole Cammie?

THE ANSWER

Katie had told Officer Krumky that she'd had late soccer practices all week—so Courtney Cresswick couldn't have seen Katie playing with Cammie the previous afternoon as Courtney had claimed. When confronted, Courtney confessed—she'd taken the kitten because she was afraid it would get into her yard and make her allergies even worse! Of course, handling the cat did in fact make her allergies worse—so much for trying to avoid sneezing! Courtney directed Officer Krumky to her older sister's house, where she'd hidden the kitten—and Katie and Cammie were reunited that night.

GUESS WHAT? There's an alternative answer to this mystery! Can you guess what it might be? Think about it, look over the story for clues, and turn to page 60 to see if you're right.

THE CASE OF THE SNEAKY SNAKE

Who snuck in and slipped off with the Slithery Sapphire?

Officers Hiss and Scales were the only patrol officers working the beat when a call came in at 6:00 P.M.—there'd been a robbery at Jake's Jewels. When the officers arrived, the front door of the jewelry store stood ajar, and Jake Snake and his assistant, Fang, were the only ones in the store.

"I called you as sssoon as I could," Jake said.

"I'm sssure you did," Officer Scales replied. "Now what happened here?"

"The Ssslithery Sssapphire has been ssstolen," Jake said, "and I sssaw the sssnake who did it!"

"Can you be a bit more sssspecific?" asked Officer Hiss.

Jake nodded. "The Ssslithery Sssapphire was the most valuable item in the sssstore—we only had it here for a few days, to polish it for the Ssslithery family. It was in this case right here." Jake motioned toward a broken display case right next to the cash register. "We'd closed for the night. While Fang sssswept the floor, I locked the front door and made sssure each display case was locked. Then I counted the cash in the register, locked it, and went in the back room to do inventory. Just after Fang went out the back door to take out the garbage, I heard a crash and came running out—my display case was broken, the sssapphire was gone, and I sssaw the back of a quick little brown-and-white sssnake making a break for it out the front door."

"Is this true?" Officer Scales asked Fang, who had coiled up in a ball next to the register.

"Yes," Fang said. "Jake locked everything up front, and I took out the trash. I heard the crash while I was out there, and I came ssslithering in, but I missed the whole thing—the sssapphire was already gone."

"Does your assistant have a ssset of keys to the front door?" Officer Hiss asked.

"No, I'm the only one with a key—Fang just sssstarted working for me on Tuesday, ssso I haven't given him his own ssset of keys yet. But Officers, I don't think Fang had anything to do with this—he's been an honest employee ssso far."

Officer Scales was skeptical. "You're going to

42

have to come down to the ssstation with us for a little while," he said.

"But I didn't have anything to do with this," cried Fang. "I promise!"

"Not you," Officer Hiss replied. "It's your boss who committed this crime."

How did the police know it was Jake who stole the sapphire?

THE ANSWER

Jake told Officers Hiss and Scales that he'd made sure the front door of his store was locked before the robbery occurred. Since Fang didn't have a key, and the door hadn't been forced open, the only one who could have stolen the sapphire was Jake. When confronted with the evidence, Jake confessed—and he let Fang run the shop while he went off to jail!

10

THE CASE OF THE DASTARDLY DOG

Who stole the Top Dog show's mystery prize?

THE CHARACTERS

Bones: *An enormous Saint Bernard*

Pugs: *A perky pug*

Harmony: *A prissy Chihuahua*

Mitzy: *A lively dachshund*

The Top Dog contest, held once a year for hundreds of competitive canines from around the world, was *the* dog show to compete in.

All day long, dozens of breeds—boxers and beagles, poodles and Pekepoos—trotted across the arena floor, hoping to win the affection of the human judges.

Of course, they also hoped to win the contest—and the mystery prize hidden behind a giant red curtain.

It all came down to four final dogs waiting anxiously backstage for the judges' decision. There was Bones, a big, friendly Saint Bernard; Pugs, a plump, playful pug; Harmony, a cute, stylish Chihuahua; and Mitzy, a smart, bossy dachshund.

"Well, I think it's quite obvious who's going to win

this year," boasted Bones. "I'm adorable!"

"We'll see about that," said Pugs. "Did you notice how they all applauded when I played dead? They couldn't get enough of me!"

"How about my sweater and matching beret, though?" yipped Harmony. "They ate it right up!"

Just then Mitzy scurried over to them, her tail wagging wildly. "I just heard the judges talking!" she said. "Someone swiped the secret prize!"

"How did someone take it without being noticed?" asked Pugs.

"I don't know," said Mitzy, pacing the

BARK BITES

➤ The Westminster Dog Show has been held every year in New York City since 1877. The only sporting event in America that's older than the Westminster Dog Show is the Kentucky Derby, which was first held a mere 20 months earlier!

➤ According to the American Kennel Club, the five most popular breeds of dogs are Labrador retrievers, Golden retrievers, German shepherds, dachshunds, and beagles. Chihuahuas come in at number eight, but pugs and Saint Bernards don't even make the top ten. Do you have one of these kinds of dogs? Do you know someone who does?

➤ We may think of dachshunds as adorable "wiener dogs," but they were originally bred to be fierce fighters. "Dachs" means "badger" in German, and dachshunds, with their short legs and long bodies, could scramble down into the ground and fight badgers in their burrows.

floor. "But it couldn't have been me. My legs are far too short to open that curtain. It must have been one of you!"

"It wasn't me," said Bones. "I'm too big to walk off with that prize unnoticed."

"And of course it couldn't have been me," chimed in Harmony. "There's no way that dish could fit in my tiny Chihuahua mouth!"

"Don't look at me," said Pugs. "I'm a watchdog. It's against my nature to steal!"

Mitzy stopped pacing and stared down her three rivals. "The judges can't award the prize until this is resolved," she said. "One of you needs to confess, and I know who it is."

How did Mitzy know who stole the prize?

THE ANSWER

*Harmony, the Chihuahua, said—quite accurately—that there was no way the **dish** would have fit in her small mouth. But there's also no way she could have known what the prize was unless she took it! Sure enough, the jewel-encrusted dish was hidden underneath a pile of sweaters in Harmony's carry case. The judges bestowed the prize on Mitzy for not only being the best pup, but a good detective, too!*

11

THE CASE OF THE SAUCY AUSSIE

Who stole Olivia Otter's luggage?

THE CHARACTERS

Olivia: *An otter from St. Louis, Missouri*

Wallace: *A wallaby from Sydney, Australia*

Kelly: *A koala from Adelaide, Australia*

It was January in St. Louis, Missouri, and Olivia Otter had decided to take a vacation in Australia to visit her dear old friend Wallace Wallaby. She had never been Down Under before, and when Wallace came to meet her at the airport when she arrived in Sydney, she was very excited.

"Oh, I'm so happy to be out of St. Louis!" Olivia exclaimed, as they headed toward the baggage carousel. "The weatherman said more snow was on the way today in St. Louis, but here I am on vacation instead—and look! Is that a eucalyptus tree?"

Wallace laughed. "Why, yes it is—welcome to Australia, Olivia! It's always nice to get away for a while," Wallace said. "And I've gotten you a room at the Marsupial

Mansion—the finest animal hotel in all of Sydney!"

"Oh, who can think about the hotel," Olivia said, as they got into Wallace's car. "I'm in a new place! With new things to see! We have hotels back home, but we don't have eucalyptus trees, or kangaroos, or . . ." She trailed off in a long yawn.

"You had a long flight," Wallace said soothingly. "I'm excited to show you the sights

of Sydney, but I think you might need a nap first."

"Oh," Olivia mumbled, "well, I guess that's . . . " And with that, she fell sound asleep with her head on Wallace's shoulder.

When they got to the Marsupial Mansion, Wallace checked a sleepy Olivia into her room and left her luggage in a neat stack on the floor by her bed.

"Good night, Olivia," he whispered. "I'll be back in the morning, after you've gotten some rest."

"Mrrrrmmph," Olivia replied, as she snuggled under the covers.

✧ ✧ ✧ ✧

When Wallace returned the next morning, however, Olivia was very much awake— and upset. "My luggage has disappeared!" she cried. "My clothes, my camera, my sunscreen—*everything* is gone!"

"I don't understand," said Wallace. "Did someone break into your room while you were asleep?"

"They must have," Olivia replied. "I was sleeping pretty

soundly—I don't even remember you putting me to bed, and the door wasn't locked."

"Let's see if whoever is in the next room can tell us anything about the crime," Wallace said, as he headed to the room next to Olivia's. He knocked on the door, but there was no answer.

"Try again," said Olivia.

Wallace knocked again. Finally, the door cracked open, and Wallace and Olivia could just barely see a koala standing inside the dark room.

"Yes?" said the koala. "What do you two want, and why are you waking me up during my nap?"

"My friend's luggage was stolen from her room," Wallace replied, "and we were wondering if you might have heard anything suspicious last night, Ms.—"

"Koala," said the koala. "Kelly Koala, to be exact, and as you can see, I was fast asleep last night—I'm a bear, you see, and I came to Sydney because this hotel is a lovely place to hibernate all winter long."

"Oh," said Olivia. "I guess she didn't hear anything, Wallace. Let's try the door on the other side of my room."

"I don't think we'll find the thief there," Wallace said. "If you knew anything about Australia, Olivia, you'd know this koala is not telling the truth."

How did Wallace know Kelly wasn't telling the truth?

THE ANSWER

Wallace knew Kelly was lying because koalas aren't really bears— they're marsupials, and they don't hibernate during the winter like real bears do. When confronted with her lie, Kelly apologized for stealing Olivia's luggage—she did it because she loved American toothpaste, and was sure Olivia would have a tube of it in one of her bags. (She did.)

GUESS WHAT? There's an alternative answer to this mystery! Can you guess what it might be? Think about it, look over the story for clues, and turn to page 60 to see if you're right.

THE CASE OF THE SHAGGY SHEEPDOG

#12

Who walked off with Farmer Jones's watch?

THE CHARACTERS

Farmer Jones: *The owner of Jones's Farm*

Shep Sheepdog: *A smart, friendly sheepdog*

Cedric Sheep: *A teenage sheep*

Sally Sheep: *Cedric's older sister*

Suzie Sheep: *A grown-up sheep*

It was shearing day on Farmer Jones's farm, and all the sheep had been herded into a pen so that Farmer Jones could shear them and spin his prize-winning yarn out of their thick, fluffy wool. In a small barn at the end of the pen, Farmer Jones was getting ready to start shearing— he made sure his shears were sharp, and then he took off the gold watch he'd won at last year's Wool Festival. He didn't want any wool to get caught on his watch, so he set it on a stool next to him.

Out in the pen was Shep Sheepdog, Farmer Jones's loyal companion and helper for many years. It was Shep's job to make sure the sheep behaved themselves and lined up properly as they waited in line to be sheared.

"*Baaaaa*—Cedric Sheep, you cut in line!" said Sally Sheep. She glared at her younger brother, who had just walked in front of her. "Shep told you to wait at the end of the shearing line, and you know it. So what are you doing trying to stand in the front of the line?"

"I've been waiting around for hours while Shep figures out the right shearing order and Farmer Jones gets everything ready," Cedric replied. "What's the big deal if I cut in here?"

Shep trotted over to Cedric and Sally, when he overheard their bickering.

"Are you two alright?" Shep asked. "I thought I heard some fighting."

Sally sighed. "No, Shep—everything is fine, that is, if it's OK for Cedric here to stand in the front of the line

instead of where you placed him at the end of it."

"Sounds fine to me," said Shep. "Now if you'll excuse me, I think Farmer Jones is ready to get started."

"First sheep!" Farmer Jones called out, and Cedric stepped up to be sheared.

Just after Farmer Jones was finishing Cedric's haircut, the animals heard Farmer Jones's voice coming from the shearing pen. "Shep!" he yelled. "Shep Sheepdog, you come here right now!"

"Wow," Shep said, "Farmer Jones sounds angry. I guess I'd better see what this is about!" With that, he ran over to the shearing pen and jumped over the fence to get inside.

When Shep reached the barn at the end of the pen, he could see that Farmer Jones's face was red with anger. "My gold watch is missing!" Farmer Jones yelled. "And you're the only animal who can jump in and out of the shearing pen whenever you want! You must have taken my watch while I was shearing Cedric the sheep!"

"But I—I didn't take it!" Shep stammered.

Farmer Jones thought for a moment. "Well, you have always been a good dog, Shep. So I'll give you fifteen minutes to prove that one of the other animals could have gotten in and out of this pen without my noticing them."

Shep walked down the line the sheep stood in. "Do any of you sheep know how I can prove to Farmer Jones that I didn't steal his watch?" he asked.

"Well," said Suzie Sheep from the end of the shearing line, "there's a hole in the fence back here, but I don't think a sheep could fit through it." She walked over to the hole and tried to push herself through, but her fluffy wool kept getting stuck. Even with the other sheep helping her, Suzie couldn't fit through the hole. "Nope," she said, "a sheep couldn't get through."

Shep and the other sheep searched the entire pen, but there weren't any other holes in the fence. Finally,

Shep gave up and walked back over to where Farmer Jones was standing.

"I don't know what to tell you, Farmer Jones," Shep said. "I swear I didn't take your watch, but I don't know how to prove it. With all that wool, the sheep are just too big to fit through the only hole in the fence. I don't know who could have gotten through."

Farmer Jones thought for a moment or two. "You say the sheep are too big to get through the hole, eh?" he said. "Well, Shep, I think I might just know who took that watch of mine. And you're telling the truth—it wasn't you."

How did Farmer Jones know who actually did steal his watch?

THE ANSWER

Suzie Sheep showed how she couldn't get through the hole in the fence, but she hadn't been shorn yet—a freshly shorn sheep would be skinny enough to squeeze through the hole. The only sheep who'd been shorn before Farmer Jones noticed his watch was missing was Cedric. Sure enough, it was Cedric, who was found by Shep two miles down the road, trying to sell the watch to a crooked mule in a neighbor's pasture.

13

THE CASE OF THE
Speedy Snail

Who snagged the cash at the Slow-and-Steady Supermarket?

THE CHARACTERS

Sergeant Slimonowski: *A snail detective*

Officer Squidge: *The sergeant's loyal assistant (also a snail)*

One night, the local police in Snailville got a call that the Slow-and-Steady Supermarket had been broken into one hour after closing.

"Well, the thief is in for a big surprise," Sergeant Slimonowski told his assistant, Officer Squidge. "The silent alarm just went off a minute ago, so he's still got to be in the store."

"Then let's go!" Officer Squidge replied. Very slowly, the police officers began to crawl toward their patrol car.

Luckily, cars move faster than snails, and Sergeant Slimonowski and Officer Squidge were able to make it to the scene of the crime about seven minutes after the alarm went off. However, when the officers arrived at the supermarket, they were wrong about catching the thief in the act. Scattered glass from a broken window was all over the sidewalk and all the cash registers in the store were empty, but the criminal was nowhere to be seen.

"I don't get it, boss—there's no way a snail could have robbed

this place in seven minutes," Officer Squidge said. "It takes me more than seven minutes just to get down the eight-foot-long hall in my house to brush my teeth at night!"

"Let's take a moment to review the evidence," Sergeant Slimonowski said.

"OK," said Officer Squidge.

"The call came in, and we answered it seven minutes later," Sergeant Slimonowski said. "There's broken glass on the sidewalk and no sign of a criminal in the store."

"True," said Officer Squidge.

"I think I know how this crime was committed, and finding the thief shouldn't be difficult at all," said Sergeant Slimonowski.

"But how?" asked Officer Squidge.

How did the Sergeant know the method used to rob the supermarket?

THE ANSWER

The Sergeant's first guess—that the robber broke in through the window to rob the store—had to be incorrect, because no snail could move fast enough to commit the crime in less than seven minutes. Therefore, the crime had to have been committed by the last snail present in the store, and the criminal had to be nearby. The police found night-shift clerk Shelly Shellington slowly making her getaway just a few blocks away.

GUESS WHAT? There's an alternative answer to this mystery! Can you guess what it might be? Think about it, look over the story for clues, and turn to page 60 to see if you're right.

ALTERNATE ENDINGS

Did you solve any of the mysteries using a different clue than the answers provided? The same way some questions have more than one right answer, some of the mysteries have more than one solution—just because a character solves the mystery one way doesn't mean you can't solve it another way! Check out some alternate solutions right here.

The Case of the Kidnapped Kitten, page 34:

When Courtney came to the door to talk to Officer Krumky, she was suffering from allergy symptoms. But people with hay fever feel better at night when pollen from the plants that bothers them during the day is no longer in the air. Officer Krumky knew that Courtney must have been in contact with something else she was allergic to—Katie's cat!

The Case of the Saucy Aussie, page 47:

Another hint for Wallace that Kelly was lying about hibernating was that Australia is in the Southern Hemisphere, where the seasons are the exact opposite of North America's. A bear in Australia wouldn't be asleep in January—she'd be enjoying a nice warm summer! Not that a koala is a bear anyway, but Kelly's bear facts were off!

The Case of the Speedy Snail, page 57:

The sergeant might have also been able to solve this crime by noticing that the glass in the broken window was scattered on the sidewalk. When a window is broken, the glass will scatter in the same direction as the object that broke it came from. Since the broken glass was on the sidewalk instead of inside the store, the sergeant must have realized that the criminal had broken *out*, not *in*.